ANNABEL LEE, P.I.

ANNABEL LEE, P.I.

AND OTHER MYSTERY STORIES
Compiled by the Editors
of
Highlights for Children

Compilation copyright © 1995 by Highlights for Children, Inc.
Contents copyright by Highlights for Children, Inc.
Published by Highlights for Children, Inc.
P.O. Box 18201
Columbus, Ohio 43218-0201
Printed in the United States of America

ISBN 0-87534-656-1

Highlights is a registered trademark of Highlights for Children, Inc.

CONTENTS

ANNABEL LEE, P.I.

By Judy Cox

It's eight-twenty in the morning. Another school day. Dad's in the kitchen grinding coffee beans. Mom's in the bedroom drying her hair. John's in the laundry room looking for clean socks. In the living room, the television is on, screaming a song about hunky-chunky cat food.

And me? I'm working the day shift out of headquarters. Annabel Lee. Private Investigator.

Call me Al. It's my initials, get it? A.L. Annabel Lee. But only my parents call me that. My friends call me Al.

"Mom!" A piercing yell from the laundry room. My superbrain identifies it at once as belonging to my older brother, John. "Mom, where's my gray sock?" Mom comes to the top of the stairs.

"Look in the dryer!" she calls.

"I did already. It's gone," John wails. "I need that sock!"

"Did you try under your bed?"

"It's not there," John complains.

"Well, if you'd only remember to put your dirty clothes in the hamper in the first place . . ." Dad pokes his head around the kitchen door. Mornings always make him grouchy.

I hear John banging around the laundry room. "This is the third pair of socks I've lost this month! We need a new dryer. I think this dryer eats socks!" he says.

Sounds like a case for Annabel Lee, P.I. I pull on my battered old slouch hat and grab my notebook. Flip it open to a clean page. Pull my new fine-point marker from over my ear. Leap downstairs, taking the steps two by two, to the laundry room. I'll interview possible witnesses.

John first. "Just the facts, sir," I tell him. "When was the last time you saw the alleged gray sock?" I lick the tip of my pen, like they do on cop shows. It tastes real funny.

John gives me a dirty look. "Last time I wore it, birdbrain." He thinks for a minute, then says, "Let's see. I wore my gray shirt to the game on Friday. Must have been then."

"Can you describe the AMS?"

"The what?"

"Alleged Missing Sock. It's what we call them," I explain patiently.

Another look from John. He dangles a long, gray, woolly object in front of me. "It's a sock, see. What do you think it looks like? An elephant?"

Honestly, big brothers are a pain. I take the object from him. "Just the facts, sir. The missing sock matches this one?"

He nods. I take the sock and write "Exhibit A" in my notebook. Next I head up the stairs to interview Mom, following the roar of the blow dryer. I show her Exhibit A. "Excuse me, ma'am. Can you identify this sock?"

"Oh, you found it? John was looking for it. Get dressed for school, dear, or you'll miss the bus."

"This isn't the missing sock, ma'am. This is its mate." I lay the sock neatly on the bed to show her. "Have you seen this sock before?"

Mom sighs. "Listen. I do laundry ten billion times a week, and if you expect me to be able to tell you where one little sock is . . ." She switches the hair dryer off. "If you and your brother would offer to help once in a while . . ." She looks in the mirror and fluffs her hair, then catches sight of me. Her eyes narrow in The Mom Look. "Annabel, I thought I told you to go get dressed."

I head downstairs to interview the head of the household. I find him at the kitchen table, reading the paper and sipping coffee.

"Sir, have you seen a sock like this? Inquiring minds want to know." I hold out the gray sock.

Dad takes it, absentmindedly. "Isn't this the sock I lost last week? Where did you find it?"

I take Exhibit A back. "Sorry sir, this is John's sock. I'm looking into the alleged disappearance of its mate."

He goes back to his paper. "While you're at it, look into the disappearance of mine. We've only got ten minutes."

"What's that?" Mom comes downstairs—every hair in place—and pours herself a cup of coffee.

"Nothing, dear," says Dad. They both look at me. "Annabel! Go get dressed!"

If I were a sock, where would I hide? I pace through the living room, looking for clues. What kind of clue could a sock leave? Footprints? A bit of unraveled wool? A sticker that says 'Inspected by No. 13'?

In the corner, the television howls about sugar-coated cereal. The sound makes it hard to concentrate. I head over to switch it off. Suddenly, there on the screen is a clue! Some man is walking down the hall, his pants all twisted up, a sock stuck to his back. The screen switches to a lady with her dress sticking to her slip and then shows a can of spray gunk for your dryer. I've got it! I click off the TV and race to the laundry room.

The gray sock is there, inside the dryer with the last load, clinging to Mom's new silk blouse. "I found it!" I yell. John comes pounding down the stairs. Mom and Dad poke their noses in from the kitchen. "Look here!" I wave the sock triumphantly.

"Solid detective work, Sis," admits John, taking the sock. He puts it on. "Now, let's have it."

"Have what?"

"My other sock. The one I gave you. Exhibit A." He holds out his hand, balancing on one foot, one sock on, one sock off. "Give it here. I need it."

I look at my hands. Notebook, check. Pen, check. No sock "Now let's see. I had it just a minute ago. . . ."

The Lost Ring Mystery

By Margaret Springer

Liam sighed. It was raining again. Did it ever not rain in England? Ever since they had gotten off the plane it had been raining.

He trudged out of the tailor's shop and along High Street behind the rest of his family. He could still feel that measuring tape around his chest.

A tuxedo was not his style, especially not one with a pink handkerchief in the pocket and a pink carnation in the buttonhole. But nobody listened to Liam.

Mom and Dad and Mike and Daphne chattered on ahead. All Mike ever talked about was Daphne. Mike, his own brother, getting MARRIED! Liam sighed again.

He shivered and looked up at the gray English sky. Rows of red slate roofs and lines of chimney pots stretched into the distance.

Ahead, Mike and Daphne stopped suddenly. Liam almost walked into them. They were kissing again.

"Come on, lovebirds," Dad said. "We'll be late for the rehearsal."

Inside, the ancient church was dark and gloomy. Liam twisted in his seat. He looked at the stained-glass windows while the rector went over the ceremony.

"This is where Liam comes forward with the ring," he said. Liam jumped up.

"Oh, yes," said Mike. He reached into his pocket. He looked embarrassed. He checked his other pockets. "I know I had it. It was there when we left the hotel. I'm sure of it."

They all helped look. The wedding ring seemed to have disappeared.

"Maybe it's outside somewhere," Liam said. "Can I look, Mom?"

"Just between here and the hotel. We don't want to lose you, too."

Liam was glad to get away on his own. He walked with his head down, searching carefully.

Now and then the sun came out, but everything looked gray and wet. He stopped beside the shiny prickles of a tall holly hedge.

This was where Mike and Daphne had stopped to kiss. He ran the film again in his head. Daphne looking up at him. Mike grinning, and wiping off the lipstick—

"That's it! Mike took a handkerchief out of his pocket. That's when the ring fell out. It has to be around here somewhere."

Liam searched the sidewalk around and under the hedge. Nothing. He peeked through to the other side. In a tiny front garden, birds chattered at a bird feeder and spring bulbs bloomed. He reached his hands through and crouched on all fours, searching grass blade by grass blade. No ring anywhere.

For almost an hour Liam hunted, until there were grass stains on both knees, and his shoes were soaaen. Maybe someone else had found the ring and taker   He hurried back to the hotel.

They went to Daphne's parents' house for tea: warm scones and sausage rolls, watercress sandwiches, and almond cakes. And tea. Lots of tea.

They phoned the police to see if anyone had turned in a ring. Nobody had.

Liam felt tired all over. He scrunched into his chair and stared into space.

"I wish this wedding were over and we could go home again," he said suddenly, not realizing he'd said it out loud

The room was quiet. Mom and Dad glared at him. Liam scrunched even lower.

Only Dapnne's father seemed to understand. "Here, come with me, lad. I'll show you our new bird feeder. You sit here, with this bird book, see, and check off what you find. You might see a dozen different species if you're sharp about it."

He patted Liam on the shoulder. "And never you mind, lad. All this wedding fuss will be over before you know it."

Liam propped the book in front of him. To his surprise, he enjoyed finding starlings, magpies, robins, and chaffinches. He counted seven different kinds of birds just while he watched.

It was the middle of the night when Liam suddenly figured it out He sat straight up in bed. "Yes!" he said out loud. But he had to wait until morning to persuade Mike to go with him.

"What's this all about?" Mike grumbled. "I have a million things to do before the ceremony. We haven't even had breakfast yet."

"I know who stole your ring."

"Stole it? Are you making this up?"

"No, honest! Come with me."

They headed back along High Street to the narrow curb beside the holly hedge.

"Magpies!" Liam said. "Those big black-and-white birds. They steal shiny things and put them in their nests."

They went to the house and rang the doorbell. Yes, the woman said, they could look around if they liked.

"They were in that bird book," Liam explained. "And I saw some in this garden when I was here yesterday afternoon."

The woman's husband brought out a ladder. It didn't take long. Inside a magpie nest, Liam found two shiny milk bottle caps, scraps of silver candy wrappers—and one gold ring.

"Well done, Liam!" Mike shouted. He gave Liam a high five.

At the reception, everyone talked about Liam and the ring.

"How are you enjoying the wedding, dear?" they all asked, over and over.

Liam didn't say that his tuxedo was suffocating him. He didn't say that he hated pink. He just shook hands, mumbled something nice, and smiled until his cheeks ached.

Even sweet milky tea and watercress sandwiches were beginning to taste OK.

"Hey, Sherlock," a boy said. "You're coming to my house afterwards. I'm one of Daphne's cousins. We can watch videos."

"All right!" Liam said. He took another cream bun.

It was raining again. But English rain was soft and gentle. Kind of nice, once you got used to it.

Turtles
and
Other Ghosts

By David Lubar

Jenny was beginning to wonder if she had made a mistake. "Maybe we should have stayed in the cabin," she told her sister as they sat near the edge of the lake. She looked over her shoulder at the small cabin on the hill. If she squinted, she could just make out her folks on the porch.

"Don't be silly," Beverly said. "We'll have lots of fun. You'll see."

"How do you know?" Jenny asked. "You've never slept in a tent."

"They always have a good time, don't they?" Beverly pointed to their brothers, who were fishing.

"I guess so." Jenny picked up a small stone and tossed it into the water. She liked to watch the ripples spread out in big circles across the surface of the lake

"Hey!" her brother Mike shouted. "You'll scare the fish."

This isn't any fun, Jenny thought. "Come on," she said to Beverly, "let's go back to the tents."

They walked through the woods to a small clearing where two tents had been set up. Beverly opened a book. Jenny got back to work on the black scarf she was making.

"You know what?" Beverly said, looking up from her book.

"What?"

"I'll bet they'll try to scare us tonight."

"Scare us?" Jenny didn't like the sound of that. "How will they do that?"

"They'll probably tell ghost stories," Beverly said.

"They wouldn't," Jenny said. But it did sound like something Mike and Robert would try. "Even if they did, I wouldn't be scared." She returned her attention to the scarf. In a few minutes, she was lost in other thoughts and forgot all about getting scared.

That evening, as they sat around the fire, Mike said, "Would you like to hear a story?"

"Thanks," Jenny said, "but I'm getting sleepy. I think I'll go into the tent." She saw that Mike looked disappointed.

"Me too," Beverly said, following her sister into the tent.

"That took care of them," Jenny told her.

"It was pretty easy," Beverly said. "That was good thinking on your part. But I'll bet they try something else. They'll probably make wolf sounds or something."

"Nothing we can't handle. Hey, listen to this," Jenny said. She could hear Robert and Mike talking outside.

"It didn't work," Mike said.

"Maybe tomorrow," Robert answered. There was a pause, then he said, "Look, there's a turtle."

Jenny heard footsteps. After that, she heard Mike say, "I have a great idea." He must have whispered, because she couldn't hear most of it. She did hear the word *hat* a couple of times and *turtle* once.

Robert laughed. "That'll scare them, all right."

"What do you think they're up to?" Beverly asked Jenny.

"I don't know. I'm not afraid of turtles. Neither are you. They must know that." Jenny wondered what they were planning. She thought about what she had overheard, and how her brothers wanted to tell ghost stories. "Listen," she told Beverly, "I have an idea. I think I know what they're going to do. Would you like to teach them a lesson?"

Beverly nodded. Jenny explained her plan.

"It will serve them right," Beverly said.

Jenny lifted the back of the tent. She felt the ground for a stone, then tossed it into the woods behind the clearing. She heard her brothers running over to see what it was. "Hurry," she told Beverly. "You don't have much time. Don't forget this," she added, handing something to her sister.

Beverly left the tent. Jenny waited. She wasn't surprised a few minutes later, when Mike called, "Hey, Jen, Bev, get out here. You have to see this."

Jenny smiled, knowing she was right. "Sshh— Beverly is asleep," she said, coming out of the tent. "What is it?"

"Over there, look over there." Robert pointed across the clearing. In the dim light cast by the dying fire, Jenny could barely make out a white object. It was Robert's fishing hat.

"Watch," Mike said, trying to sound mysterious.

Slowly, the hat started to move. "It must be a ghost," Robert said. "Aren't you scared, Jenny?"

It was hard for Jenny to keep from laughing. She watched the hat. As she had expected, her brothers had put it on top of the turtle. *Some ghost*, she thought. The hat moved right next to a large tree. Here was the moment she was waiting for. "I'm not scared," she told them. "I like ghosts."

Her brothers didn't say anything. They were staring at the hat, which had started to rise from the ground. When it was several feet off the ground, Robert asked Mike, "Turtles can't climb trees, can they?"

Mike didn't answer. He started backing toward the tent. "What's the matter?" Jenny asked. "Don't you like ghosts?" She knew her brothers were about to have a bigger surprise.

Then it happened. The hat vanished. It just popped out of sight. Mike and Robert looked at each other and then turned and ran to their tent. Head first, they dove through the opening.

Jenny couldn't hold it back any longer. She ran to the tree and started laughing. Beverly, still behind the tree, was laughing, too.

"You should have seen their faces," Jenny said.

"That will teach them a lesson." Beverly lowered the hat. When her brothers were in the woods, she had tied fishline to the hat and looped the line over a branch. From behind the tree she had been able to raise it without being seen. From the distance, the boys didn't notice that the turtle was still on the ground. "The last part was a great idea," she said. "How did it look from over there?"

"Perfect," Jenny told her. "It looked just like the hat vanished. Poof—it was gone." She took the black scarf back from Beverly. Her sister had tossed it over the hat from behind the tree.

"Should we tell them the truth?" Beverly asked.

"Tomorrow," Jenny said. On the way back to the tent, she told her sister, "I changed my mind; camping can be fun."

The Mysterious Sound

By Helen Kronberg

"Ready, Adam?" Doug called.

Adam got his fishing pole from the garage. "I hope we catch something for a change," he said.

Doug laughed. "Maybe the moose is scaring them away."

Adam scratched his head. "I can't figure out that sound. My dad thinks it must be a loon."

"No way," Doug said. "We both know what a loon sounds like. This sounds like a moose. Well, I think it sounds like a moose."

Adam put his bait can on the riverbank. He chose a worm and baited his hook. "Have you ever seen a moose?"

"I saw one in a movie once. It sounded a lot like the sound we've been hearing."

"Only there aren't any moose around here," Adam reminded him.

He chewed his tongue as he reeled in his line. "Oh, nuts!" he said. "I thought I had one." He looked at the remains of his bait. "I guess I did—for a minute."

He started to rebait his hook. He jerked to attention. "There it is again."

Doug stood with his mouth open. His fish line lay slack in the water.

"Sounds like it's on the island," Adam said.

Doug nodded. "But not exactly in the same place as yesterday."

"How would a moose get to the island?" Adam said. "Especially when there aren't any anywhere in the area."

"It would sure make a mess of all Mr. Hopkins's gardens. Have you ever eaten any of the stuff he grows? My mom thinks it's great." Doug wrinkled his nose. "Actually, some of it's not too bad. Not if you like strange fruits and vegetables like rutabagas and nectarines."

Adam reeled in his line. "Let's go over and take a look."

Doug grinned. "What if Mr. Hopkins chases us off? He's not too friendly to uninvited guests."

"That's only because of his work," Adam replied. "But we're not going to trample anything. Besides, if there's a moose over there, he's got bigger problems than careless people."

They got oars and life jackets from the boathouse. "What are we going to do if we see it?" Doug asked. "We'd better not tangle with a moose."

Adam laughed as he fastened his life jacket. "We hightail it out of there," he said. "But at least we'll know what the thing is."

"We should tell Mr. Hopkins," Doug said.

Adam untied the boat and pushed it into the water. "Mr. Hopkins isn't deaf. If there's a moose on the island, he knows it." He frowned as he got aboard. "Come to think of it, we'd better make sure he's all right."

"Yeah." Doug picked up the oars. In no time they were across the river.

They tied their boat to the island's dock. Mr. Hopkins's boat bobbed on the water. "He must be home," Doug said, speaking softly.

Adam nodded. "What direction would you say the sound was coming from?"

Doug thought a moment. "I think that way." He nodded toward the right. "Take it easy," he said. "We don't want to spook it. You never know what a wild animal will do if it gets spooked."

The boys walked softly onto the island. They looked carefully from right to left.

Soon they stood on the edge of an orchard. "It sure doesn't look like there's been any damage," Adam said. He squatted and looked at the ground. "No hoofprints either."

Just then the sound split the air again.

"That sounds like it came from near the house," Doug said. "Maybe we better go back and get help."

"Help?" Adam scoffed. "We don't know yet if anyone needs help. Come on."

They walked through the orchard. There were gardens and bushes. As they neared the house the boys slowed down. "Stop puffing," Adam whispered. "A wild thing could hear you a mile away."

"We could see farther if we climbed that tree," Doug whispered.

Adam nodded. "Good thinking."

They looked around, then dashed for the tree. "I wish I had my binoculars," Doug said.

Adam touched his arm and pointed. Mr. Hopkins was working in a garden near the house. "At least he's OK," Adam said.

The boys jumped as the sound exploded once again. "Wow! That was close," Doug said.

Mr. Hopkins turned. He spoke, but the boys couldn't hear what he said.

Doug gulped. "It sounded like it's right behind him. And he doesn't even look scared."

Suddenly, a small boy burst into sight. He put something to his mouth. Out came a loud call of a moose.

Doug and Adam looked at each other. They laughed, then they scrambled out of the tree and ran to the garden. "Hi, Mr. Hopkins," Adam called. "We've been hearing that noise and got curious. We even thought you might be in danger, here alone."

Mr. Hopkins chuckled. "Hello, boys. Actually, I am in danger. I'm in danger of losing my mind, listening to Larry blow on that moosecall. I'm sorry I ever let him have it. He is my nephew, by the way. Larry, meet Doug and Adam."

Mr. Hopkins wiped his face with a bandana. "Larry is staying with me for a couple of weeks. The trouble is, I just haven't had time to entertain him."

Suddenly he laughed and picked up his hoe. "Larry, why don't you give the boys some lemonade. You know where all the games are kept. Set up the croquet set, volleyball net—whatever you want. Maybe that moosecall wasn't such a bad thing after all."

The Graffiti Mystery

By Susan Mondshein Tejada

Margaret McCarthy threw the scrub brush to the ground and kicked it across the narrow alley. "It's not fair!" she cried. "Someone else makes a mess, and I have to clean it up. Again!"

She stamped her foot, but that didn't make the mess go away. She walked over and picked up the brush. With a sigh, Margaret finished scrubbing the graffiti off the warehouse wall.

The graffiti had first appeared at the beginning of summer. Margaret had gone out on the balcony to water her mother's plants. Then she saw it.

Across the alley, on the wall of the warehouse behind her apartment building, someone had painted the words: MR. LEMBO IS A CREEP.

Mr. Lembo was the best superintendent her apartment building had ever had. Margaret knew the words would hurt his feelings. So she grabbed the scrub brush and a pail of soapy water and ran downstairs. As fast as she could, Margaret washed the paint away.

But that wasn't the end of the graffiti. The mystery painter struck several more times. He scrawled a line saying all the girls on the block were dummies, and another saying all the boys smelled bad. He wrote that the grocer on the corner sold rotten food. Each time new graffiti appeared, Margaret scrubbed it away.

One hot night toward summer's end, Margaret couldn't sleep inside the stuffy apartment. She went out on the balcony. *At least there's a breeze outside,* she thought.

Suddenly she heard a noise below. Margaret peered through the balcony railing. It was the graffiti artist! His back was toward her, and he was spraying paint on the warehouse wall.

When he finished, he turned to run away. As he passed under a light, Margaret got a good look at his face. She had never seen him before. The next morning she was outside early, scrubbing the mystery painter's words away.

School began a week later. There was a new student in Margaret's class. His name was Nick, and he had moved from another part of the country. The teacher asked him to stand up and introduce himself. Margaret turned to listen.

Her heart began to pound. Nick was no stranger. She had seen him before. Once, on a hot summer night.

On the way home from school that afternoon, Margaret spotted Nick walking ahead of her. She caught up with him at the corner.

"Stop!" she cried, grabbing his arm. "I'm Margaret. I'm in your class. I know you."

Nick smiled. "Yes, I met you in school."

"No," Margaret said sternly. "I mean I already know you."

Nick looked puzzled.

"The graffiti," Margaret said accusingly. Now Nick looked frightened.

"How could you paint those cruel things about everyone?" Margaret asked. "And what did Mr. Lembo ever do to you? If he saw those words, he would have felt terrible."

Nick sank to the curb. "So you're the one who

washed everything off. I'm glad you did. I never should have painted all those things."

"Then why did you do it?" Margaret asked.

"I don't know," Nick muttered. "I was homesick, I guess. We had just moved. I didn't have any new friends, and I missed my old friends. I got the paint, and you know the rest. It was stupid. I wish I had never done it."

Margaret knew by the look on Nick's face that he was telling the truth.

"Well, Nick, since we're going in the same direction," she said, "let's walk home together."

As they walked, Nick told her about his hometown on the coast. Margaret had an idea.

"Nick," she said, "if you miss your home so much, and if you like to paint, why don't you paint a mural on the warehouse wall? I can help you. We can paint all the things you're telling me about—the waves, the beach, the lighthouse, everything! Mr. Lembo has leftover paint, and I'm sure he'd let us use it."

Nick and Margaret ran home. When they explained their plan to Mr. Lembo, he said he'd be happy to give them the extra paint. Then he called the owner of the warehouse, who liked the idea of a colorful mural decorating the wall.

That night Nick made a small sketch of the

mural. The next day, right after school, he and Margaret got to work.

Margaret told her friends about it, and they told their friends. Everyone wanted to help paint the mural. Nick made so many new friends that sometimes he forgot to miss his old friends.

Every day Nick and Margaret and the other kids painted in the alley. One crisp afternoon in late October, they finished.

The picture of a summer day in Nick's hometown stretched from one end of the warehouse wall to the other. The sun shone on a lighthouse and a rocky shore. Nick's old friends played on the beach. There, in the middle, was his father's old sailboat.

Mr. Lembo gave a block party to celebrate. "What a beautiful mural!" he exclaimed. "Now it will always be summer in our alley."

Margaret whispered in Nick's ear while everyone clapped and cheered. She promised never to tell anyone that she had solved the graffiti mystery. She promised to keep the secret always. And she did.

THE MYSTERIOUS Birthday Present

by Rosalyn Hart Finch

After school Sally went to her little brother Teddy's room. His head peeked out from under the quilt on his bed. "Do you feel better today?" she asked.

"My head aches, and I'm sad because I have chicken pox on my birthday," Teddy replied.

"I'll read you a story," Sally offered. She was only about halfway through when Teddy fell asleep.

Quietly, Sally tiptoed downstairs. "Mom," she said, "I don't have money to buy Teddy a birthday present this year."

"Make something," Mother suggested.

"Like what? I want to give Teddy something special this year because he's in bed with chicken pox that he caught from me."

"Think about your special talents, and maybe something will come to you." Mother smiled. "While you're thinking, please take the garbage outside to the can first."

"OK." Sighing, Sally picked up the garbage bag and went outside. Shivering, she tried to hurry over the ice-crusted snow and slipped. Down she went, spilling eggshells everywhere. As she gathered them up, she noticed a little dab of egg yolk had dribbled onto the snow, making bright yellow spots. Suddenly Sally shouted, "I know what I'll make Teddy!"

The rest of the afternoon Sally was busy running up and down the stairs and in and out of the house. Once she hurried to Teddy's room. "May I borrow your red paint?" she cried.

"What for?" Teddy demanded.

"I need it for your surprise birthday present."

"What is it?"

Sally smiled. "If I tell you, it won't be a surprise!"

"Is it big?" Teddy questioned.

"Yes, quite big," Sally answered. She rummaged in Teddy's art box and pulled out a plastic jar marked "Red Tempra." She grabbed a paint brush from his desk, then ran downstairs.

Later, when Teddy heard her downstairs, he called, "Come here a minute, Sally."

Sally zipped upstairs again. "What do you want?"

"Is the surprise soft or hard?" Teddy asked.

Sally grinned. "Well, it's soft and also has some hardness to it."

"How can that be true?" Teddy grumbled.

"You'll see, Teddy." And Sally clattered back downstairs. Soon she was back. "May I borrow your brown gloves, Teddy?"

"Are they for my present, too?"

"Well, not exactly, but my mittens are making it too hard for me. Gloves would work better."

Teddy frowned. "OK, you can use my gloves."

"Don't worry. It's one of your favorite things," Sally promised.

"I know!" Teddy cried. "You're making me brownies, and you're wearing gloves so you don't get chocolate on your hands. The paint is to decorate the wrapping paper. Brownies are soft before baking and a little hard afterward."

"But brownies aren't big," Sally reminded him. She took the gloves from Teddy's drawer.

"Why are you going outside and inside so much?" Teddy questioned. "I can hear you."

"Some stuff for the present is outside." Sally sped away.

When Sally came upstairs the next time, Teddy cried out, "You're making ice cream from snow the way Grandma did, right?" Teddy laughed. "You need my gloves to gather snow, which is soft at first then hard when it becomes ice cream. My red paint is for my birthday card."

"Wrong!" Sally giggled. "I don't know Grandma's recipe. Besides, ice cream isn't big."

"I give up!" Teddy grumbled.

"Here's a great clue—animals are in it," Sally said. Teddy looked puzzled.

A little later Teddy heard Sally calling, "Mom, where is the flag on a pole that we had?"

"It's in my closet," Teddy shouted.

Sally came up to get the flag, and Teddy yelled, "You're making me a doghouse for the dog I'm getting this Christmas! A doghouse is big! And made of hard wood. But the sleeping blanket inside is soft! The red paint is to print his name over the door. And you're wearing my gloves to keep from getting splinters and hammer-hurts on your fingers. The flag will fly on top. Hurry up! I can't wait to see my doghouse!"

"I'm sorry, Teddy, but it's not a doghouse," Sally declared, shaking the flag as she scampered away.

Before Teddy had time to think up more ideas, Sally was back. "Teddy, if you feel good enough to walk to Mom's and Dad's bedroom, you can see your present now," Sally said.

"I do!" Teddy shouted.

At their parents' bedroom door, Sally ordered Teddy to close his eyes. She led him inside and seated him on a chair. Then she called, "Turn it on, Mom!"

Immediately the sound of marching-band music filled the house.

"Open your eyes, Teddy," Sally commanded.

Teddy's eyes flew open. He was seated at a window overlooking the backyard.

"Look down," Sally cried.

"Wow!" Teddy shrieked. "It *is* my favorite thing!"

Below, on the hard, icy top layer of snow, Sally had painted a big, bright parade with the red paint. The parade leader was a tall, red clown pulling a wagon full of balloons with one hand and holding a flag in the other. Behind him was a long line of dogs and cats of all shapes and sizes. Next came a bumpy elephant with a dancing girl on his back. Following them were two boys on bikes, and behind the boys was a car stuffed with teddy bears. A red fire-engine and four horses with monkeys on their backs came next, with a whole group of children marching at the end of the parade holding up a sign saying HAPPY BIRTHDAY, TEDDY!

"That's really something!" Teddy cried happily.

"Parades need lots of red so I had to borrow your paint. It's big! And the snow is icy hard on top and soft underneath. I could paint better with your gloves on than with my mittens. The clown leader is carrying that flag. So now you understand the mysterious present," Sally said, "with animals in it."

"Right!" Teddy agreed. "Thanks a lot, Sally. But how did you ever think of painting on snow?"

"A little egg yolk told me so," Sally said mysteriously.

The Great Paper Chase

By Linda White

"Not again!" an anguished voice cried.

Candice dropped her mystery book and did three cartwheels down the hall, red braids flying. She landed squarely by the phone as her older brother slammed the receiver down.

"Someone's stealing newspapers," Tim shrieked. "I deliver them all, but people call saying they didn't get one. I could lose my job!"

"Just what I've been waiting for, a real case!" Candice disappeared, returning shortly with Dad's old briefcase, now labeled "Detective Case." She pulled out a neatly lettered card and handed it to Tim.

He stared at it for a moment, then said "I don't know, Candice, my job is at stake."

"What have you got to lose? I can stake out your paper route every afternoon. You can't. You have basketball practice."

"Guess you can't make things any worse. OK, see what you can do."

"You won't be sorry." Candice pulled out a pad of paper and pencil. "Tell me what you know about the theft."

"Nothing. I deliver the papers. Then some of them disappear, all from our block."

"How many are missing?"

"At first, one or two. Yesterday, nine!"

"Don't worry. I won't quit this job until the case is solved."

"If that's not pretty soon, you'll have to tell the next paperboy."

After school the next afternoon, Candice grabbed the detective case and stationed herself in a big juniper bush in the front yard. From there, she could see the whole block. Squinting through the binoculars and checking her watch, she made notes:

Case 1

Missing papers, day 1

3:00 Twins Muffy and Mitzy Taylor dawdle by on their way home from school.

3:07 Mrs. Smith goes to Larson's to feed the dog, Smokey. Lets him out in backyard.

3:10 Mrs. Smith goes home.

3:21 Chris Orosco arrives home, shoelaces dragging as usual.

3:37 Neighborhood people come and go. Nothing unusual.

3:48 Tim reports all papers delivered. Juniper bush scratchy. Move to Mom's van.

4:02 Suspicious stranger in trench coat approaching on foot. Will follow.

4:30 Stranger used key to enter house two blocks away. Probably walked home from work.

4:38 Back to van. Mrs. Smith looking in bushes. Oh no! Her paper is gone!

Talked to Mrs. Smith as she went to Larson's to put Smokey back in. She saw nothing. Neither did other neighbors. No strangers, nothing unusual at all.

Seven papers missing. Bought more, delivered to injured parties. Tim's job protected for today. Checked scenes of crime for evidence. None found. Absolutely none.

"Sorry I followed that man," Candice told Tim later. "That's when the papers disappeared."

"He could have been the one," Tim replied. "I'll pay you back for the extra papers. You didn't buy one for the Larsons, did you? Mark said not to deliver one while he and his parents are in Chicago taking care of his grandmother."

"I didn't, but while I was at the store, I saw a poster for a paper drive. The one who turns in the most wins a portable CD player. I'll check to see if anyone has turned in a bunch of unopened papers. I will find the thief."

The next afternoon, Candice was again on duty.

Case 1

Missing papers, day 2

3:00 Pouring rain. All quiet. Twins got ride.

3:10 Mrs. Smith runs to Larson's under torn umbrella. Gets soaked. Smokey dashes out, does business, runs back.

3:12 Mrs. Smith runs home, minus umbrella.

3:45 Tim reports delivery finished. Nothing unusual. Stakeouts are uncomfortable.

4:00 Neighborhood people come and go. No one picks up paper other than his or her own. How do detectives stay awake?

4:45 Mr. Jenkins arrived home last, picked up his paper. None missing today.

While doing the dishes, Candice and Tim discussed the case.

"It wasn't the stranger in the trench coat," Candice said. "And the man at the paper drive hadn't noticed anything suspicious. I hate to say it, but it almost has to be someone in this neighborhood."

"Why do you think the papers disappeared five days in a row but not today?" Tim asked.

"Well, it is raining. Maybe the thief doesn't . . . Wait, I know who did it!"

"Just like that?"

Candice laughed. "You won't believe who. I'll show you tomorrow. We'll catch the thief in the act of stealing papers."

"Well, Nancy Drew," Tim said the next day when he finished his route, "show me the thief."

Candice pointed to the Larson's fence. "Mrs. Smith just let Smokey out and went home. Watch."

There was a rustling in the bushes and Smokey popped up. He ran to the Smith's house, grabbed their paper and dashed back home, diving through a hole under the fence.

Candice and Tim ran to the Larson's backyard. Smokey sat happily wagging his tail, aglow in a pile of newspapers.

"A real newshound!" Candice said, stroking the dog's big head.

"I could have lost my job because of you, Smokey," Tim said, petting the dog. "How'd you know it was him?"

"The papers didn't disappear until the Larsons had to leave town. The only day there were no missing papers was when it rained, and Mrs. Smith didn't leave Smokey in the yard. Then I remembered seeing Mark teaching him to retrieve sticks. Whenever he did, Mark gave him a treat. He must think he's earned a whole box full of dog biscuits by now."

"Good job, Sis. You've saved my job and solved the Case of the Dog Gone News."

Treasure
in the
Desert

By Marianne Mitchell

Luis unlocked the heavy wooden door and pushed it open. Sunlight invaded the dark interior of the old adobe house. The cluttered room looked the same as always, except that Don Sebastian wasn't there to greet him. Luis blinked back his tears. He didn't want to be there.

Luis glanced at the *ristra*, a string of dried chiles hanging by the door. Their musty smell filled the air. How his grandfather had loved those chiles! Luis ran his fingers over the dusty table that took up most of the main room. It was piled with books, papers, and letters. One of the letters caught his eye. It was addressed to him.

As Luis stared at the envelope, his brow wrinkled. Why was there a letter for him? He hardly noticed when his parents lumbered into the house carrying boxes.

"Look at this place!" said his mother. "Don Sebastian never threw anything away. It'll take us days to pack all this up."

His mother always called his grandfather by his formal name. Luis called him *Abuelo*.

"What's that you have, Luis?" asked his father.

"It's a letter for me. I found it on Abuelo's table."

"Well, aren't you going to read it?"

Luis tore open the envelope. "This is weird," he said. "It's from Abuelo. What does this mean?" Luis read aloud:

> A treasure chest I leave to you
> It's hidden safe and sound
> But you're a clever boy, it's true,
> And soon it will be found!

His mother laughed. "Even though Don Sebastian has died, he's still up to his old tricks! He loved to play hide-and-seek with our presents. He said it was more fun than just handing them to us."

"Guess he's left you something valuable, Luis. But you have to find it," said his father.

Luis looked around at the piles of Abuelo's things. "It'll take forever! And I don't even know what I'm looking for!"

"Don Sebastian's most valuable possession was his coin collection," his mother said. "He started it as a boy. I'd bet that's what he left you."

"We have to pack up everything anyway," said his father. "The house will have new owners next week. I hope you find your treasure before then."

Luis started his search in Abuelo's bedroom. First he poked around in the battered chest of drawers. Then he looked under the bed. Nothing but dust balls there He tugged the mattress to the floor. No luck. He felt behind all the books on the bookshelves. This was harder than he thought.

His mother and father filled box after box with Abuelo's things. Clothes and kitchen items would go to the mission shelter. Furniture and sentimental items would come home with them. Everything was checked carefully.

By evening they had cleared away most of the clutter. A big pile of trash waited by the door, spoiling the beauty of the nearby cactus. They sat around Don Sebastian's old wooden table eating take-out chicken for dinner.

Luis reread his mysterious letter a dozen times, looking for a clue. "A treasure chest . . ." Could that mean a big box? "Hidden safe and sound . . ." Did Abuelo have a safe? Luis scanned the smooth adobe walls. Nothing looked like a place for a safe. He looked at the envelope. The stamps were very pretty.

"Are these stamps valuable?" Luis asked. His father studied them under the light. "Nope. They're nice, but not old enough. Don Sebastian also put way too much postage on that letter."

Luis looked at the stamps again. One thirteen-cent stamp had a picture of an adobe house, like the one they were in. Next came a twenty-cent stamp with a saguaro cactus on it. After that was a diamond-shaped stamp, worth ten cents, that showed a picture of petrified wood. The last stamp read "Banking and Commerce." It was worth ten cents, too. Fifty-three cents for a thirty-two cent letter. It wasn't like Abuelo to waste money.

Money! Luis stared at the last stamp, the "Banking and Commerce" one. The design was all coins. He banged the table with his fist. "I know where the treasure is! These stamps are telling the story. See, this is like Abuelo's adobe house," said Luis, pointing to the first stamp. "This saguaro cactus must be the one near the door."

Luis dashed outside. Sure enough, a tall saguaro loomed dark against the sunset. He looked down at the base of the cactus. He knew what he would see. A huge chunk of petrified wood sat nestled in the dirt. He tugged at the heavy stone until he had pushed it aside.

His mother brought out a small shovel, and it wasn't long before Luis and his mom unearthed a heavy metal chest. Inside, hundreds of shiny coins—silver dollars, Indian-head pennies, and others—winked up at him.

Off in the distance, Luis heard the *yip-yip-yip* cry of a coyote. He looked up from his treasure and smiled. "It sounds like Abuelo is laughing at me out there."

"Yes," said his mother. "If he were here, he'd be having a good chuckle over how he made you search. You must have inherited his brains as well as his coins. He knew that you would figure out the message!"

Flying Ghosts

By Virginia L. Kroll

A cicada utters one last, long buzz, and the sun-singers hush in the rustling trees. A nighthawk screeches the twilight in. The wind dies down. A steady hum fills the air, like an orchestra tuning before it explodes.

Suddenly, my sister's voice cuts through the stillness. "A ghost!" she shrieks. "A ghost!"

"Now Nancy," I say, "you should know that there's no such thing as ghosts." I'm older, so I know these things.

"Is too. I saw it with my very own eyes." She is panting. "Flew right out of the old red barn, right over my head. It even screamed at me in a weird, hissing way," she says. She sounds so sure that I begin to wonder. She continues, "Go see for yourself if you don't believe me."

"I'll go with you," I offer.

She agrees so I let her lead the way.

We hear peepers chirping from the gravel pit as we walk around the pond nearby. Two white-cheeked geese honk tiredly and hunker into the reeds. They freeze when they hear our footsteps. We finish circling the pond and pause. The crickets stop their *chirriping* as if they know something we don't.

"Let's go. You promised," Nancy says.

I take a step. A shadow flits in front of me. I jump and grab my sister's arm.

"It's just a bat," she says. "Now who's afraid?" We watch the bat and try to guess how many mosquitoes it gulps on its zig-zag hunt.

"Coming?" I ask after a while.

The longer we walk, the darker it gets. The old red barn looms ahead up the hill, looking like a haunted castle. It's used just for storage now, ever since the new one with the matching silver silo went up.

"Closer," Nancy says.

We sneak up on the old red barn and edge over to the honeysuckle bush. Slowly, we sit.

Time goes by. Fireflies blink silent signals, calling each other with glowing rhythms. A katydid rasps and another one answers.

"Frogs, crickets, even quarreling katydids," I say, "but no ghosts. Told you." I stand up and brush the grass from my pants.

Something hisses over my head. Zips so fast that all I can see is a huge white blur. Another hiss. Another white blur. It brushes my forehead

"Ghosts!" I gasp.

Nancy and I take off down the hill. The ghosts come after us, screaming above our heads. Our screams turn into hoarse croaks. Are our feet even touching the ground?

My heartbeat pounds in my ears *such things as ghosts, such things as ghosts.* My throat burns, and I feel dizzy.

We reach the pond. Nancy slips and slides into the reeds. I skid and flop down next to her We flush out the geese, but they don't scare us because they're geese. Our breaths are gasps.

We lie there silently, listening, long after our breathing is easy again.

"Has it been long enough?" Nancy wonders.

"They're gone," I hope out loud.

We get up slowly and look all around. Then we are off again.

Our house welcomes us like a warm hug. We fall into the cushiony armchair together and sink in as far as we can go. Mama hollers from the kitchen, "Where have you two been so late? Get washed up for snack. Carrot cake tonight."

We scrub the dirt from our hands and faces, but the grass stains stay. Our clothes are damp. We shed them and slip into our cool, flowered night-shirts and go back downstairs. We still haven't said a word.

We nibble our carrot cake and sip our milk. Our eyes dart back and forth from window to window. Mama says, "What have you two been up to? You sure have the heebee-jeebees tonight." She goes back to her chores.

We say good night, run upstairs, and jump into our double bed.

"It's hot," Nancy whispers.

"I know," I whisper back.

We push close together and pull the sheet up past our chins. We listen, wide-eyed.

"Where did they come from? Why do you suppose they're after us?" Nancy asks.

"Don't know," I say. "Don't want to know either."

"Hear anything?" Nancy asks.

"Frogs, crickets, katydids," I say. And there is Mama's humming and the screen door creaking to let Papa in.

"But . . . ?" Nancy whispers.

"No," I say, hoping I am right.

Papa stops at our door and rubs his back. He has just milked our sixty cows. The smell of hay tickles our noses. "Hi, little ladies," he says. "Listen, I want you to steer clear of the old red barn for a while. There's a pair of big white barn owls nesting there. Go anywhere near their territory when they've got young'uns, and they'll go after you like screamin' demons. 'Night, girls." His shadow follows him down the hall.

"Barn owls!" We exhale together.

Now it is our turn to hoot and howl. Our laughter bounces off the walls and flies out through the screens.

"Girls! Hush!" Mama's voice whooshes over us like a cool breeze.

We put our laughter into our pillows until it stops coming out of us. Then we listen to the whispers of the night, and the moon spills its silent light over our sleepy heads.

SECRET
OF THE
SPARROW

By Steven J. Sweeney

We found the first wood carving in our tree house—Tom's and Brian's and mine. The house looked out over the cedar fence behind my yard, into the timothy hayfield, and across to the railroad tracks.

One leafless branch hung like an elephant trunk over the fence, so anyone walking the dirt path on the other side could climb up and tightrope over to the tree house ladder. I figured that was how the wood-carver got in. It took a lot longer to figure out why.

The guys showed up first thing Saturday, same as always, and we headed for the tree house. We had a good setup: a padlocked cupboard, a pair of old binoculars, our club flag, even a wool army blanket left from a camp-out. Brian reached for his camouflage cap as we climbed in. But all he grabbed was air.

"Hey, what's the deal?" he asked. "Where's my cap?" He looked around. "Where's my jacket?"

Only a length of chain hung on the pegs, the kind with wooden links that carvers might whittle from a single piece of birch.

"I didn't know you were so sharp with that pocket knife," said Tom, lightly punching Brian's arm.

"I want my stuff back," Brian complained.

"Relax. You probably wore it home last time and forgot," I told him, though I doubted it. I looked the chain over. The link on one end joined a small cage. Trapped inside was a ball carved round and smooth as a marble.

"Someone left this here," I said, as if Tom and Brian couldn't figure that out for themselves.

"Brilliant, Einstein," said Tom, tapping his head. "Hey, let's eat." He patted his shirt pocket. "I brought peanut butter crackers."

We watched the freight as it sidetracked a couple of hopper cars for the granary. Sometimes when the trains moved slowly, we'd see men climb into empty boxcars. My father thought a few might be farmers cut loose by the drought. Other folks said they were bums running from steady work.

We couldn't do anything about Brian's stuff. We forgot about it until the next week, when the army blanket disappeared. That grabbed my attention because it was my dad's. I stared at the spot where it had been and where a carved figure of a bear now rested, a salmon in its jaws. I could tell it was a salmon, that's how good the carving was.

Brian smirked. "You probably wore it home last time and forgot."

"We need a plan," I said.

After supper, we made excuses to be out after dark. We met behind my dad's shed and waited. Not for long.

Though the night was calm, leaves in the tree suddenly shivered with moonlight. A silhouette snaked along the branch to the tree house. I nudged Brian to hush, and he reached to flick Tom but hit the metal shed instead. The person in the tree froze—then disappeared.

"Come on," I ordered.

We scrambled through the corner gate and down the footpath. Over toward the railroad trestle we saw a faint, flickering light. Keeping low, we zigzagged across the hayfield until we could see into the clearing around the trestle.

A man sat in the middle near a small fire. He spoke in a foggy, low voice to a boy who stood nearby with his head down. Someone who was huddled on the other side of the man rose suddenly and looked in our direction.

I guess we all saw the knife at the same time. Tom and Brian sprang up out of the grass and flew off like pheasants flushed out on a hunt. I crouched, breathless.

The army blanket hung on the boy's shoulders. Behind the man, Brian's hat and jacket almost hid a girl with thick, reddish braids. Above the firelight, their faces looked more scared than mine.

It's OK, I wanted to say—to myself, maybe to those people by the trestle. I don't know if I actually said it. I took a few steps back, turned, and ran home.

I couldn't sleep. Sometime after midnight, I took my backpack to the kitchen. In went soup cans, crackers, a package of licorice, anything that would keep. I slipped out and left the pack in the center of the tree house floor.

At dawn, I went back out barefoot in the dew-wet grass. I climbed far enough to see that the pack was gone. In its place was a sparrow, wings outstretched, each turn of its feathers carved so exactly I thought I'd surprised a real bird in the tree house.

I dropped a couple of rungs and saw him, the boy from the night before, backpack slung over one shoulder. At least I think I did. I hardly more than blinked, and he vanished.

Later that day, near the trestle, we found the ashes from the fire, surrounded by the kind of chips you make when you whittle with a knife.

That all happened last fall. The wooden sparrow hangs in the east window of my room now. Some mornings when the sun hits it just so, it seems alive. I often wonder, if the sparrow could fly, would it know where to look for the people from the trestle? Would it find them in a good, warm place?

The Mystery
of the
Lost Letter

By Carolyn Kane

"Exactly what did Grammy write in her diary?"
Annie asked her twin brother, Kevin.

"Just that she was cleaning out her grandfather's
desk and found a letter signed 'A. Lincoln.'" He
read aloud from the tattered red diary: "I can't
believe this is a real letter from Abraham Lincoln,
because the penmanship is even worse than
mine. But just in case, to keep the letter from getting lost or stolen, I've put it in the box with the
wedding rings."

Annie glanced around the living room of the fine old lakeside home that had once belonged to her grandmother, the house where the family would be staying for the summer. Her eyes rested on the secretary where Kevin had found the diary. The old desk was packed with books and bulging with old papers.

"Didn't Lincoln usually sign his letters 'A. Lincoln' instead of 'Abraham'?" she asked. "And didn't he write with a scribble?"

"That's what Mr. Grant said in history class last year!" Kevin sounded excited. "If we could find that letter, we'd be guaranteed to win first prize at the History Fair next year, and we'd probably get an A in history, too."

Annie ran her fingers through her hair as she thought aloud. "Grammy said she put the letter in a box with some wedding rings. That means a jewelry box."

"I'll bet it's in the attic!" Kevin said, jumping to his feet. "History Fair, here we come."

The attic was a pile of boxes, trunks, old books, toys, worn-out board games, and suitcases. "So many boxes!" Annie said. She opened a hat box and found a black velvet hat with a broad brim and a long feather. She ran her finger along the feather and then set the hat on the floor, planning to try it on later. She opened a bread box, which turned out to be jammed with doll clothes.

Kevin sneezed as he opened a large chest. "Nothing here but some old quilts," he said. "Have you found a jewelry box?"

Annie was standing on a chair to reach the top shelf of the closet. "Yes, a big one. Come help me!"

They got the box down, opened it, and began taking out costume jewelry—cameo pins, brooches in the shape of owls and elephants, clattering necklaces that were heavy with artificial rubies and diamonds. At the end of a long chain, a golden peacock spread its jeweled tail. Annie slipped the chain around her neck and held an owl-shaped pin against her sweater.

"Too bad these jewels aren't real," Kevin said. "We could buy the school and give ourselves an A in history." He shrugged. "Well, no sign of a letter from Lincoln or anyone else. Want to try the basement?"

In the basement they found a trunk full of old clothes, a box of buttons and thread, and a chest of tools, but no jewelry boxes. "What about the desk?" Annie said. She started taking books out of the drawers. "Look! Grammy's old Girl Scout Handbook and her school books! Grammy never threw a book away, did she?" Then her hands touched a box. "Kevin, I think I've found it!" Kevin grinned at his sister as she drew out a small wooden box, beautifully painted with blue and white flowers. It was the right shape to hold a letter.

Annie opened it carefully. Tissue paper was folded inside "I think there's some kind of jewelry in here,' she said. "Something round and gold—"

'Wow! Granddad's gold watch!" Kevin exclaimed. "It's been lost for years!"

The twins looked at each other. "Well," said Annie, "we've found the watch, which will make Mom and Dad happy, and we've found enough stuff to open our own antique shop."

"If we want an A in history, I guess we'll have to get it the old-fashioned way—study," Kevin said. "But I think we must be forgetting something. Look, we didn't know Grammy very well, but we do know she was smart, right?"

"Dad says she was the smartest person he knew."

"She wanted to hide the letter where it wouldn't be stolen. Now think: if you were a burglar, where's the first place you'd look for something valuable to steal?"

"In the china cabinet where the silverware is, of course, or in—in a jewelry box."

"Right! Would our brainy grandmother pick such an obvious place to hide a valuable letter?"

"No," Annie admitted. "We've forgotten something, but what?"

Even in the summer, the lakeside house grew cold after dark. That night Annie went upstairs to her room, crawled into bed, and settled underneath her red-and-blue patchwork quilt. She loved the cool nights and the warm bed, but tonight she could not fall asleep. Visions of shiny rings began to swirl in her mind. *Whose wedding rings?* she wondered. *Where would you put a wedding ring except in a jewelry box?* A cool breeze ruffled the curtains, and Annie snuggled under the quilt, enjoying its warmth and softness.

Suddenly she sat up in bed. Wedding rings— quilts—a box! She sprang out of bed and tiptoed to her brother's doorway.

"Kevin? Are you asleep? I think I know where the missing letter is. Didn't you find some old quilts in the attic?"

"Yes, in the big wooden box at the foot of the bed, but—"

"That's where the letter is. Come on."

"But what do quilts have to do with anything?" asked Kevin as he followed his sister upstairs.

"It's what we forgot!" Annie opened the box and unfolded a white quilt that was covered with patches in bright, bold circular patterns. "There's a kind of quilt called a 'wedding ring!' We're going to get that A in history after all—and get our pictures in the paper when we hand this letter over to the museum." Carefully she felt between the folds of the quilts and pulled out a folded piece of yellowed paper.

The
Dancing Puppets

By Diane Burns, Clint Burns, and Andy Burns

"Whoa," Bernard said in a low voice. Nina and the wooden wagon slowed to a stop in Clearwater's empty town square. Bernard looked around sadly. So it was true. Clearwater had become a ghost town in the year since his last visit. It happened sometimes in these frontier mining towns When the mines closed, the townspeople moved on.

The horse's ears pricked forward. Nina had expected children to come running, to scratch her soft belly and to squeal, "Oh, it's the puppet master and Nina!" But there were no children. There was no laughter. There was no sound at all in the thick August heat.

It was too late in the day to travel farther. Bernard undid Nina's harness, letting her graze in the overgrown grass. He braced the wagon wheels with stout rocks, then lowered the caravan's wooden side shutter. Inside were his beloved marionettes, staring at him with their painted eyes.

The large wooden figures hung by sturdy wire strings tied to their stiff joints, the whole dangling row attached to the ledge above the shutter. During each show, Bernard hid on that upper ledge. When he pulled the marionette's wires, his hand-carved family danced with joy.

They would not dance tonight. He and Nina were alone. As he did whenever he was lonely, Bernard touched his wooden puppets lovingly. How he longed, sometimes, to cuddle a friend without wires!

Bernard opened the food box strapped to the side of the wagon. He took a chunk of boiled fish from its oiled paper. He sat in the shade of the gaily painted wagon that was his home on wheels. First he would finish his supper and enjoy

a cool drink from the spring that had given Clearwater its name. Then he would fetch his mandolin
from the wagon seat and play a song or two.

Swallowing a bit of the boiled fish, Bernard
glimpsed a movement inside the wagon. He
stared, unbelieving. The wagon was still. The air
was still, yet the puppets were quivering by themselves. They were dancing on their wires!

Bernard glanced around uneasily. Was this the
work of a ghost in the new ghost town?

Hurriedly, Bernard jumped to his feet. His heart
pounded. It was no mistake. The puppets were
jiggling for no reason at all. As Bernard watched,
the dancing marionettes slowed until they dangled
silent and unmoving once again. They smiled at
him with the same painted smiles they always
wore. Bernard's thoughts whirled. How could
there be such mystery in a deserted town?

Ping! Twang!

His mandolin! Bernard hurried over to the
wagon seat. The mandolin lay there, untouched.
But he hadn't imagined the sound. The mandolin
had played music. Bernard scratched his head.
Puppets that moved by themselves. A mandolin
that played music by itself. Never before had such
things happened.

Clickety-clack! Clatter!

The puppets were beginning another dance. Quickly, Bernard ran to the back of the wagon and climbed inside. A face, dainty and whiskered, peered down at him.

Bernard laughed. His "ghost" was nothing more than a half-starved calico cat! Bernard held out a morsel of his fish, and the cat came eagerly.

"Little Ghost," Bernard whispered, stroking his visitor. "You skittered across the ledge and made my puppets dance. You jumped across my mandolin strings and made music."

Little Ghost just purred.

"Poor kitty," said Bernard. "Did they leave you behind when they moved away? Do you need a friend like I do?"

As if she understood, the cat licked Bernard's fingers with a warm, rough tongue. Then Little Ghost scrambled to Bernard's shoulder, where she snuggled against his neck. Deep, throaty purring shook her skinny body.

Something inside of Bernard was purring, too.

TOO SCARED TO SLEEP

By Nancy Lenz

Beth heard an owl hoot and the night wind rustle through piles of dead leaves. She shivered and unrolled her sleeping bag near a big oak tree.

"This is a good spot to spend the night," Kelly said. "I'm glad your uncle said we could sleep out on his land."

"Maybe we should be a little closer to the cabin," Beth answered.

"What's the point of camping out if we sleep next to the cabin?" Kelly asked.

"Promise you won't be too scared to sleep out if I tell you?" Beth said.

"Tell me what?"

"Uncle Frank said to be sure to fasten the gate so the ghosts won't come in."

Kelly laughed. "Hey, you don't believe in ghosts, do you? You know how your Uncle Frank is always kidding around. I think he was just teasing you."

"Maybe," Beth said. She shivered. It was getting dark fast. Already the cabin was lost in the shadows of the forest behind it.

They took off their boots and slid into their sleeping bags. Beth turned on her flashlight and let the light shine along the fence. She could see that the gate was shut tight. *Of course, Uncle Frank was just kidding about the ghosts,* Beth thought. That was just like him. He was trying to make sleeping out a real adventure.

Kelly yawned. "It's pretty late," she said, using her flashlight to look at her watch in the fading light. "I'm going to sleep."

Beth lay still. She heard the steady sound of Kelly's breathing. She heard the sound of wind in the trees. Then she heard a noise by the gate. Her heart beat faster. She turned the flashlight in that direction. Something white moved on the other side of the gate.

The gate rattled. Something white was trying to open it.

"Wake up, Kelly!" Beth shouted, reaching over and shaking her by the shoulder. "There really are ghosts!" Beth's flashlight picked out two white forms near the gate.

"Let's get out of here!" Kelly yelled.

The two girls squirmed out of their sleeping bags and ran to the cabin, leaving their boots and sleeping bags behind. They locked the cabin door behind them.

Uncle Frank found them sound asleep, sitting in chairs and wrapped in blankets, when he brought down doughnuts early the next morning.

"What goes on here?" he asked. "Your sleeping bags are out under the oak tree, and here you are asleep in the cabin."

"Oh, Uncle Frank," Beth said. "The ghosts came, just like you said. We saw them!"

"Ghosts?" Uncle Frank shook his head. "I never said ghosts would come!"

"You did so," Kelly said. "You said be sure to fasten the gate so the ghosts couldn't get in. We saw two white ghosts over by the gate last night. That's why we ran in here."

Uncle Frank laughed. "I didn't say *ghosts*. I said be sure to fasten the gate so my neighbor's *goats* wouldn't come in. They're always trying to sneak into my vegetable garden. Look outside."

Beth and Kelly groaned, then they began to laugh. There by the fence stood their two hairy, four-footed "ghosts," calmly chewing grass.

The Mystery of the Missing Fish

By Carolyn Short

A scream ripped the air as Trey stepped out of the huckleberry bushes. It sounded like—his heart skipped a beat—Steve! Had he seen a bear? Fallen into the ocean? Trey raced for the spot where he'd left his cousin. What could have happened? He'd only been gone for a few minutes. Trey ran faster. Had Steve caught a shark? Been stung by a jelly-fish? There were so many things that could have happened to an eleven-year-old kid from Cincinnati, who was visiting Alaska for the first time.

Trey heaved a sigh of relief when he saw Steve, apparently unhurt. "What's wrong?" he shouted.

"It's gone!" Steve yelled.

"What . . .?" Then Trey noticed the empty tide pool at Steve's feet. When he'd left, his cousin's magnificent fourteen-pound salmon had nearly filled the pool. How could it have disappeared? Who would have taken it? Trey stared into the empty pool. He always kept his salmon in tide pools until it was time to go home, so they'd stay cool. He scratched his head. "But, weren't you right here?" he asked his cousin.

"I went to get my camera," Steve explained. "When I got back my fish was gone."

"Why didn't you take it up to the house with you?" Trey asked.

"I don't know," sighed Steve, kicking a stone into the pool. "Now, none of my friends will believe that I really caught such a huge fish."

Trey patted his cousin's shoulder. "Maybe we can find it."

"How?"

"We'll look for tracks."

"But there are rocks around this pool," protested Steve. "How can there be tracks?"

"Whoever took it had to come from somewhere," Trey said. He pointed to a sandy area of the beach beyond the rocks. "You look on that side," he instructed his cousin, "and I'll look on this side."

Steve halfheartedly began to search his area. He followed along the line of seaweed and debris swept in by the last high tide. Suddenly, he shouted, "I found some!" Trey dashed over. He bent down to examine the tracks. One set belonged to a large dog and the other to a child with medium-sized feet.

"Jason and Moby?" Steve asked. Trey nodded.

"But I passed them on my way down here," Steve said. "They didn't have my salmon."

"They might know something," Trey said. "Let's ask." The two boys scrambled up the bank and headed for Trey's house. They found Trey's younger brother, Jason, seated at the kitchen table, eating chocolate chip cookies. His big black labrador, Moby, sat beside him, his head resting on Jason's lap.

"Jason, did you take Steve's fish?" Trey asked.

Jason swallowed. "You mean that big salmon that was in the tide pool?" Trey nodded. "Not me," said Jason, reaching for another cookie.

"Then who?" Trey asked, covering the top of the cookie jar with his hand. He stared down at his little brother. "I think you know something," he said. "Who took the fish?"

Jason gulped and glanced at the dog. "Moby did," he said. "But I put it back."

"When did Moby take my fish?" Steve asked, glaring at the big black dog. "Where did he take it?"

Jason wiped his mouth on his sleeve. "Moby didn't take it anywhere. He grabbed it, but I took it away from him. I put it right back into the tide pool. Honest."

"Did you put it back in the same exact tide pool?" Steve asked.

"Of course I did," Jason answered, sliding off his chair and scooting out of the room. Moby trailed behind him.

"Maybe he didn't," Trey whispered to Steve after the two had left. "Let's look around." The boys quickly searched the beach but they didn't find the salmon.

Steve hurled a rock into the ocean. "Who could have stolen the best fish I ever caught?" he muttered. He plopped down on a large rock. Trey sat beside him. They watched the tide inch its way up the beach. "Where could it have gone?" Steve moaned. "Who would have taken it?"

Trey could think of nothing to say that would make his cousin feel better. He tried to think of all the possible culprits. They'd seen no people or animals on the beach that day. Suddenly, he became aware of a sound he hadn't heard before. Piercing, creaky cries came from the far side of a nearby point. "C'mon," he said, leaping to his feet. "I think I know what might have happened."

They sprinted across the beach toward the point. When they got there, they plowed their way through salmonberry and huckleberry bushes. Just before reaching the beach, Trey crouched behind a moss-covered stump. His cousin squatted beside him. Not more than twenty feet away, they saw three eagles gathered around the carcass of a large salmon, tearing off chunks of meat.

Steve gasped. "My salmon?" Trey nodded and held his index finger to his lips. He pointed to the camera hanging from his cousin's neck.

Steve aimed and snapped a picture. "Now I have proof," he whispered. Then he frowned and said, "My friends are never going to believe this story. I can hardly believe it myself."

"It doesn't matter," Trey whispered. "Every good fisherman has a story about the one that got away. In this case, you won't be making it up."

Steve watched as the eagles gulped down the last of his salmon. Then, he smiled. "You're right," he said. "I can't wait to tell my friends this story!"

The Peach Thief

By Joette Rozanski

I smiled at Mr. Johnson as Janie and I passed his house, but he didn't smile back. Instead, he got up from his porch swing and came down to the sidewalk.

Mr. Johnson is a big, quiet man. His blue jeans and T-shirt were dusty and grass-stained, so I knew he'd been working outside. He frowned down at us, and his thick eyebrows touched each other.

"Debbie, Janie," he said in his growly voice. "You kids can't hang around here anymore. No more shortcuts through my backyard."

Janie scrunched up her eyes and wrinkled her nose. She was going to start crying any second. But I was ten years old, too grown up to be scared. As Janie's big sister, I had to take care of her.

"What's wrong, Mr. Johnson?" I asked.

"Someone's been taking the peaches from my tree," he said. "You kids are the only ones who cut through my yard."

I knew about Mr. Johnson's peach tree. He'd planted it from a single pit, watered it, and fed it special tree food. It grew quickly, and now it had wrinkled brown bark and beautiful green leaves. Mr. Johnson was very proud of it. This was the first year the tree had grown peaches. So far, they were small and not quite ripe.

Nobody would want to eat unripe peaches. I told that to Mr. Johnson.

He shook his head. "You kids always come back from Mrs. Witt's house at six o'clock. Well, I was in my yard last night at that time. I expected you any minute. The telephone rang and I went inside the house. When I came out, three peaches were missing."

"But we couldn't eat them, Mr. Johnson."

"You didn't have to eat them. Maybe you just wanted to throw them around. Anyway, you can't come through here anymore."

He walked away before I could say a word. Janie and I had to take the long way home.

Two days later, Mom took me to the grocery store to help her do the shopping. While she looked for cereal, I stayed by the cart.

"Hello, Debbie." Mrs. Johnson stopped and smiled at me.

"Hi, Mrs. Johnson. Is Mr. Johnson still angry?"

Her smile faded. "He's not happy. Two more peaches are gone. Only three are left. I don't think you kids have anything to do with it, but he won't listen to me."

She walked away. I was sorry, too, but I had thought of a plan. Janie and I would catch the real thieves. We would prove we weren't peach-nappers.

"We're going to get in trouble," Janie said.

"No, we're not," I told her. "We're going to get ourselves out of trouble."

That evening we hid in the wooded lot beside Mr. Johnson's yard. I had my instant camera.

Six o'clock came and went. This was the time for the peach thief to show himself. Or herself.

Janie grabbed my arm. "Look!" she gasped. "A rat!"

I looked over at Mr. Johnson's yard. There was no rat, only a big old possum. It had dirty white fur and a long pink tail. It scurried across the grass straight toward the peach tree.

The possum clawed its way up the bark and out along the only branch that still had peaches on it. When the possum opened its skinny snout, I could see lots of pointed teeth inside. The mouth stretched wide and grabbed a peach.

Glomp, smack. The possum made a lot of noise as it ate. I started snapping pictures.

I heard a rustle behind us, and someone touched my shoulder. I squeaked and turned around. Mr. Johnson looked down at me.

"I've got you now!" he said. "Little thieves!"

"But . . . but," Janie said, pointing at the tree. "Look over there."

Of course, the possum had fled. But the instant pictures had fallen at my feet. Janie picked them up.

"There's the real thief!" I shouted.

Mr. Johnson looked at the pictures. Then he glanced up at us. "Kids," he said, "I'm sorry. I should have known it wasn't you."

Mr. and Mrs. Johnson took us out for ice cream. Mr. Johnson told us that he was going to put a fence around the tree.

"Too late for now," he said, "but there's always next year."

At the ice-cream store, Janie and I ordered the same flavor: peach.

We both felt we deserved it.

THE TRACKERS

By Ruth A. Sakri

Mom stormed into Rob's room the minute she got home. "Were you playing ball in the house this afternoon?" she demanded. "Did you break the living room window?"

"No, Mom," Rob protested. "After school I came straight upstairs to finish this detective book."

"Detective stories," Mom sighed. "You know I think they're a waste of time. But forget that for now. Let's go check that window."

They hurried downstairs. Sure enough, there was a round, jagged hole in one window. Cracks zigzagged away from it. Pieces of glass were scattered on the carpet. Rob took a quick look and said, "The ball came from outside. See? All the bits of glass are inside."

"I didn't notice," Mom said. "Well, let's find that baseball." She began looking under furniture.

Beside the coffee table Rob found a round, wet spot on the rug. "Mom," he said, "Look here. I don't think there's any baseball. This looks like a melted snowball."

"Hmmmm," Mom said. "I think you're right."

Rob touched the wet carpet. "It's still cold," he said. "So this didn't happen long ago. Let's go look around outside."

They threw on their coats and checked the front yard. A snowstorm the night before had dropped heavy, wet snow everywhere, and their boots made a scrunching sound as they searched. There was a bare spot where someone had scooped up snow. Mom looked at the footprints leading from it. "I'd say these prints belong to someone your age," she said.

Rob nodded, but he was studying two prints in particular. They were right behind the scooped-out spot. "This is where the person stood," he said. "And see? The right print is deeper than the left one."

Mom just looked puzzled, so Rob explained. "When you throw hard, you balance yourself. You lean on the foot opposite your throwing arm."

Mom nodded slowly. "Good thinking," she said. "The right print is deeper, so the thrower was left-handed. But who would break a window and just walk away?"

"Run away," Rob said, following the prints. "Look. There are no heel marks, because . . ."

". . . Because people run on their toes," Mom finished. Rob grinned. Mom was doing some good thinking, too.

They followed the prints. But something about them puzzled Rob. He said, "Funny, the right prints still look deeper than the left."

"And the left ones are blurry," Mom added. "The person was limping."

"It looks like that," Rob agreed.

All at once the footprints stopped and the snow was scuffed up.

"Here's another funny thing," Rob said. "Here's one handprint and one kneeprint."

"Maybe he fell down," suggested Mom.

"Most people would land on both hands and both knees," Rob said. Then he stared at the handprint. There was a band around the pinky finger. "The person was wearing a pinky ring!" he exclaimed. Then he thought for a moment as Mom kneeled to take a look at this new clue.

"It wasn't a he, Mom, it was a she," Rob said.

Mom blinked with surprise. "A girl?" she said. "Well, I guess you must be right. But why would she kneel down here?"

Rob examined some tiny tracks nearby. "A squirrel!" he announced. "It ran back and forth to that tree about ten times. And here's the reason." He picked up a peanut.

"She was kneeling down to feed a squirrel," Mom said.

"Right!" Rob's face lit up. "It was Jennie!" he exclaimed. "She always carries peanuts for the squirrels. Last summer she was our best pitcher— a leftie. The mystery is solved!"

"Good!" Mom said. "Now we should probably talk to her parents."

"Or to Jennie," Rob said. "I think she'll show up very soon. Here's her house key in the snow."

They didn't have to wait long. Soon a girl approached, searching the snow left and right. "Jennie!" called Rob. "We found your key!"

Jennie was astonished, so Rob explained every-thing. Then he added, "The only thing I don't know is why you broke our window."

"It was an accident," Jennie groaned. "I thought

you'd hear the snowball and come out to play. But I threw too hard. When the glass broke, I got scared and ran. Then I decided I had to tell you. I was on my way back to your house when I discovered I'd lost my key." She looked at Rob's mom and said, "I have enough money saved to fix the window."

Mom said, "I'm glad you're so honest. We'll talk about it later, but right now we'll cover the window with a piece of cardboard."

Jennie looked very relieved. They all said goodbye and went home.

After Rob taped the window, he went to the kitchen. Mom was starting supper.

"Can I help?" Rob offered.

"You've done plenty of work for one afternoon," Mom said. She looked at him thoughtfully. With a little smile she said, "I'm surprised to hear myself say it, but I think you should go finish that detective story."